THE STORY OF KRISHNA

MALA DAYAL has been involved with developing, editing and writing material for children for over forty years. She is the author of *Nanak: The Guru* and *The Ramayana in Pictures*, both published by Rupa.

JAGDISH JOSHI is among the best known illustrators of books for children. He has won several awards, including the prestigious Noma Concours for the picture-book *One Day*. He has also illustrated the popular book *The Ramayana in Pictures* (Rupa).

THE STORY OF
Krishna

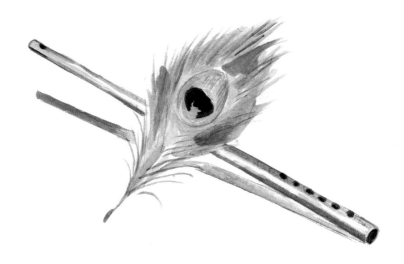

text by
Mala Dayal ❧ Jagdish Joshi
illustrated by

RED TURTLE
RUPA

Published in Red Turtle by
Rupa Publications India Pvt. Ltd 2015
7/16, Ansari Road, Daryaganj
New Delhi 110002

Sales centres:
Allahabad Bengaluru Chennai
Hyderabad Jaipur Kathmandu
Kolkata Mumbai

Text copyright © Mala Dayal 2015

Illustration copyright © Jagdish Joshi 2015

ISBN: 978-81-291-3576-6

First impression 2015

10 9 8 7 6 5 4 3 2 1

The moral right of the author has been asserted.

Printed at Lustra Print Process Pvt Ltd.

For Naina
with love and with thanks

This is the story of Krishna. Our story begins long, long ago in the city of Mathura, ruled by a wicked king called Kansa. Kansa's sister Devaki was married to Vasudeva. One day, when Kansa was driving them home in his chariot, the sky became dark and there was thunder and lightning. Suddenly, a voice rang out, 'O Kansa, Devaki's eighth child will kill you.'

Find the conch

Hearing this, Kansa put Devaki and Vasudeva in jail and, one by one, killed six of their children.

Look for the bird

The seventh child, a girl, was carried away, and escaped. Kansa was told the child had vanished.

Devaki's eighth child was born at midnight. It was raining heavily that night. Lightning flashed and thunder roared. Suddenly, Vasudeva heard a voice say, 'Take the child to Nanda in Gokula.'

Putting the child in a basket, Vasudeva walked to the river Yamuna. The waters of the river parted and made a path for him to cross over to the other side. A golden snake went with him, spreading its hood and protecting the child from the rain.

Count the sea creatures

When he reached Gokula, Vasudeva put his baby son next to the sleeping Yashoda, Nanda's wife, and picked up her baby girl. Then he walked back to Kansa's palace and gave the baby girl to Devaki.

When Kansa heard of the baby's birth, he rushed to kill it. But the child slipped out of his hands and rose up in the air, saying, 'The one who will kill you is alive.'

Can you find the baby?

Yashoda and Nanda named the baby Krishna. Kansa, always scared that the one who would kill him was still alive, sent spies everywhere to look for him. Among these, he sent a demoness, Putana. 'Kill the child and I will reward you well,' Kansa told her.

So, one day, Putana came to Yashoda's house. She picked up the child and began to feed him. No one knew that Putana's milk was poisoned. 'Now the baby will die,' she said to herself.

But the baby sucked and sucked. He sucked so hard that he sucked the life out of Putana.

Having failed with Putana, Kansa sent Sakatasura, a winged demon, to kill Krishna.

One afternoon, when Krishna was sleeping, Yashoda put him in the shade of a cart full of pots. Sakatasura took the form of a big bird and perched on the cart. The cart tilted and the pots fell on the baby. But baby Krishna was not crushed. He kicked the cart away! The cart broke and Sakatasura died under it.

Then came yet another demon, Trinavarta. He came in the form of a mighty whirlwind.

Krishna was playing outside when it suddenly grew dark and he was lifted by the whirlwind high into the sky.

Krishna wound his arms tightly around the demon's neck and pressed his throat hard. The demon tried to shake him off. But Krishna would not let go till the demon dropped down dead.

How many cows are there?

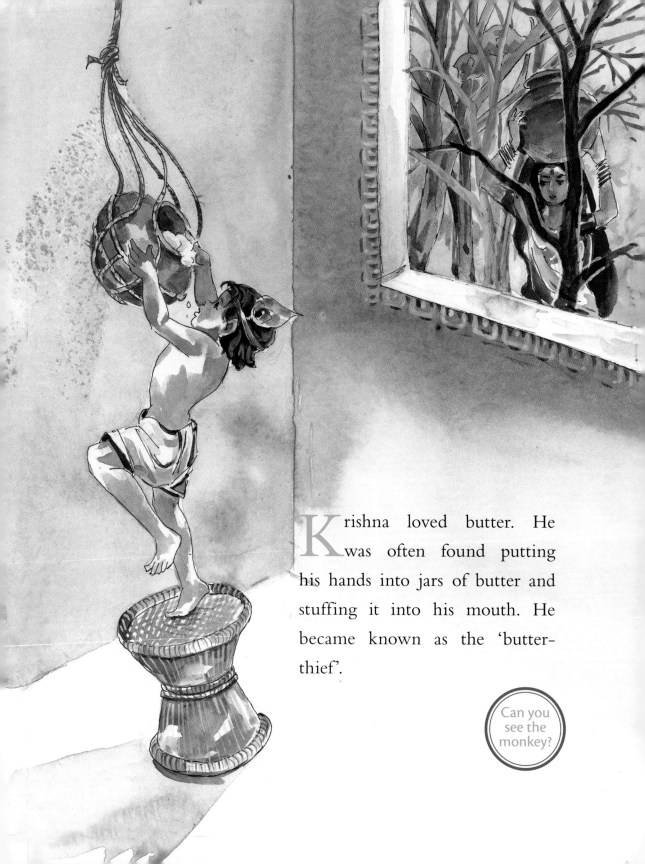

Krishna loved butter. He was often found putting his hands into jars of butter and stuffing it into his mouth. He became known as the 'butter-thief'.

Can you see the monkey?

Look for
the two
birds

To keep Krishna out of mischief while she attended to her housework, Yashoda once tied him outside with a rope to a heavy stone mortar. But the child crawled out of the gate, dragging the heavy stone behind him. Crawling further, Krishna reached a pair of tall trees growing close together. He crawled between the two trees but the stone got stuck between them. Krishna crawled on, pulling the stone. The heavy stone uprooted the trees which crashed to the ground.

Krishna was now a young boy. He had many friends but his brother, Balarama, was his closest friend. They were always together.

Count the animals

Krishna's other close friend was Radha. She loved being with him and listening to him play his flute.

Because of the constant threat of Kansa, the cowherds of Gokula decided to move to Vrindavan and settled there. Every morning, the milkmaids would go off with their pots of milk and butter to sell these in Mathura. Krishna liked teasing them and playing pranks on them.

Once, when the milkmaids were bathing in a river, Krishna hid their clothes on a tree. When they discovered that their clothes had disappeared, they were very angry. But Krishna just laughed.

Can you see Krishna?

One day, the cowherds went further down the banks of the Yamuna where the river was deep. In its waters lived the king of snakes, Kaliya. His poison was so powerful that it could kill anyone who touched it.

How many hoods does Kaliya have?

Krishna called out to Kaliya. There was no reply. Krishna called out again. Only a loud hissing answered him. Krishna jumped into the water. And do you know what happened? Krishna came out of the water dancing on Kaliya's heads!

Finally, Kaliya begged for mercy. His wives and children, too, begged Krishna to spare their king. 'Go, and never come back,' Krishna said.

Kaliya and his family swam away and never came back.

Meanwhile, Kansa did not give up his attempts to kill Krishna. One day, he sent for a demon, Vaka, who could take the shape of an animal or bird. Disguising himself as a giant crane, Vaka stood in a marsh catching frogs. Krishna came near the crane to take a closer look.

Suddenly, the crane picked up Krishna in its long, sharp beak and flew high in the sky.

Climbing on to the bird's back, Krishna held its neck tightly.

How many creatures can you spot?

'Let me go,'cried Vaka, but Krishna tightened his hold till the bird flew down to earth and fell down dead.

Even after failing so many times, Kansa did not give up his attempt to kill Krishna. Next, he sent the eight-mile long serpent-demon, Aghasura. His open mouth looked like a vast cave. As soon as Krishna, Balarama and their friends entered his mouth, the demon snapped it shut, trapping the children inside. Krishna started growing in size—he grew and Grew and Grew till he tore the demon's mouth open, killing him instantly. Again, Kansa's attempt failed.

One of the most popular festivals in Vrindavan was the one celebrated in honour of Indra, god of rain and thunder. It was important to keep Indra happy or he would stop the rain from falling, the land would become dry, and people and animals would starve and die.

But Krishna said that one should not worship anyone out of fear. He said that they should pray to Govardhan hill instead, where their cows grazed. So the cowherds went to Govardhan hill and prayed.

This made Indra very angry. He decided to teach the cowherds a lesson. The sky grew dark and it began to pour with rain. It rained and rained and rained. There was water everywhere.

The people were filled with fear. Would they drown in this rain? Would their cattle drown? The people begged Krishna for help.

And, Krishna did help. He lifted up Govardhan hill and held it on his little finger. The people and their cattle took shelter under the hill.

It rained for seven days and seven nights but the cowherds of Vrindavan were safe.

Finally Indra had to admit defeat. The rain stopped and the sun came out.

Name the animals on the hill

Kansa decided to have a festival in his capital city, Mathura, and invited people from far and near, including Balarama and Krishna, for it. He organized wrestling matches and other sports as part of the festival. He planned to use the occasion to kill Balarama and Krishna.

Everything was ready for the festival. Kansa had placed an enormous bow at the entrance to the palace. No one could lift it. But Krishna not only picked up the bow but bent it till it broke in two.

Can you spot Krishna?

I n front of the palace grounds, Kansa had kept the fierce elephant, Kuvalayapida, who had the strength of a thousand elephants. The elephant charged at Krishna and Balarama. Grabbing its trunk, Krishna lifted it up, swung it in the air and dashed it to the ground. The elephant died instantly.

Can you see Krishna's flute?

In the wrestling ring waited the king's giant-like wrestlers, Chanura and Mushtika. First, Krishna faced Chanura. Chanura tried to grab and crush Krishna several times, but Krishna always managed to slip out of his grasp. The match went on and on. Finally, Krishna flung the mighty Chanura to the ground and killed him.

Kansa then signalled to Mushtika. Mushtika was about to strike Krishna from the back when Balarama leapt into the ring and held Mushtika's neck. Balarama and Mushtika fought fiercely and Balarama defeated and killed Mushtika.

Kansa shouted to his soldiers, 'Kill the two boys! Kill them!' The soldiers rushed at Krishna and Balarama. But Krishna ran up to Kansa, knocked off his crown, caught him by his hair and pulled him to the ground. Then, taking hold of Kansa's sword, he cut off his head.

On hearing of Kansa's death, his friend, the powerful king of Magadha, Jarasandha, swore revenge. Jarasandha was not only strong but had a boon that no weapon, no disease, no poison and no accident could harm him. He would only die if the different parts of his body were torn apart and could not come together.

To escape Jarasandha's anger, Balarama and Krishna were sent to study to Maharishi Sandipani's hermitage. Krishna was a quick learner and was good at every sport. He was especially good at throwing the charka, the discus.

At the hermitage, Krishna's special friend was Sudama. Sudama was poor. He did not have expensive clothes or jewels. But these things did not matter to Krishna. They were close friends and shared everything.

Jarasandha was determined to kill Krishna, so Krishna and Balarama finally decided to move to the west. They travelled long distances till they reached the sea and decided to settle there.

On the shores of the sea, Krishna, now leader of the Yadavas, built a new and beautiful city— Dwaraka. He married princess Rukmini and princess Satyabhama.

Sudama, Krishna's friend, heard that Krishna was now rich and famous. Sudama, however, was still poor. He and his family often did not have enough to eat. Sudama's wife urged him to go and visit Krishna. 'He could help you,' she said. But Sudama always refused.

Finally, unable to see his children go hungry, Sudama decided to visit Krishna. As he was leaving, his wife gave him a small cloth bundle with parched rice. 'You always said your friend loves parched rice,' she reminded him.

The guards at the palace in Dwaraka looked at Sudama's clothes and bare feet and would not allow him to enter. But Sudama was insistent on meeting Krishna.

To the courtiers' amazement, Krishna came running as soon as he heard Sudama's name. Krishna embraced Sudama and seated him on the throne beside him. He offered him the best of food and drink in beautiful dishes of gold.

Then Krishna said, 'Do you remember how you shared your parched rice with me when we were students? I really loved it. You haven't brought any for me, have you?'

Sudama was too embarrassed to bring out his small cloth bundle. Krishna took it from him gently. 'You have brought my favourite food!' he cried happily. 'Thank you, my friend, thank you.' And Krishna ate every grain with great enjoyment.

Can you spot the bundle of parched rice?

Sudama did not tell Krishna how poor he was but, when Sudama returned home, to his surprise, instead of his hut stood a beautiful palace. Krishna had fulfilled Sudama's wishes without his asking.

News reached Krishna of the problems between the Kauravas and their cousins, the Pandavas. Krishna was both friend and adviser to the Pandavas. He told them that to make their position stronger, they must defeat Jarasandha of Magadha. He asked Bhima, the second Pandava brother, known for his strength, to challenge Jarasandha to a fight.

So Bhima challenged Jarasandha to a wrestling match. Day after day they fought, with neither Bhima nor Jarasandha winning. Finally, Krishna made a sign to Bhima. Following Krishna's secret sign, Bhima tore Jarasandha's body in two and threw the two halves in opposite directions. Now they could not join together. Thus Jarasandha died.

Find Krishna

Shishupala, prince of Chedi, was jealous of Krishna. His mother, Krishna's aunt, begged Krishna, 'Forgive my son even if he insults you a hundred times.' Krishna agreed.

Shishupala came to Indraprastha, the Pandava capital, for a ceremony. At the ceremony the place of honour was given to Krishna. This made Shishupala very angry. He flung insult after insult at Krishna. Unmoved, Krishna counted each insult.

When Shishupala had insulted him a hundred times, Krishna asked him to stop. But Shishupala flung yet another insult at him. Then, Krishna threw his discus at Shishupala. The discus flew through the air and cut off Shishupala's head.

Duryodhana, the eldest of the Kauravas, was determined to become king of Hastinapura. He knew he could not defeat his cousins, the Pandavas, in battle so he invited Yudhishthira, the eldest of the Pandavas, to a game of dice.

Yudhishthira was very fond of gambling but he lost everything he had, one after another, in the game of dice. He even lost his four brothers. He then gambled away himself. He lost and, like his brothers, became Duryodhana's slave. Finally, trying to win back everything, he promised away his wife Draupadi—and lost her too.

Draupadi was dragged before Duryodhana. To shame her, Duryodhana ordered that her clothes be pulled off. Draupadi cried out to Krishna for help.

And, a miracle occurred! As Draupadi's clothes were pulled off, they were replaced by more clothes... and more, and more, one after another. Krishna had come to Draupadi's help.

The Pandavas were set free but their troubles were not over. Duryodhana challenged Yudhishthira to a second game of dice. Whoever lost would have to go into exile for thirteen years and spend the last year hiding in disguise. If found out, they would have to spend twelve more years in exile.

Yudhishthira gambled again, and again he lost. So the Pandavas had to go into exile.

Can you name everyone in the picture?

As agreed, the Pandavas spent twelve years in exile and the thirteenth year in disguise. It was now time for the Kauravas to return Indraprastha to the Pandavas. But Duryodhana refused.

Krishna went to see the Kauravas on behalf of the Pandavas to persuade them to give the Pandavas some land and avoid war. But Duryodhana did not want peace. In fact, he told his brother to tie up Krishna. Again a miracle occurred! When they came to tie Krishna up they could not get to him for he was everywhere!

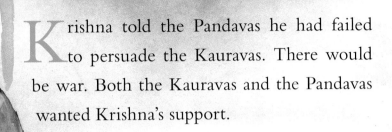

Krishna told the Pandavas he had failed to persuade the Kauravas. There would be war. Both the Kauravas and the Pandavas wanted Krishna's support.

Duryodhana and Arjuna both went to Krishna's palace to ask for his help. Krishna gave them a choice: they could have either his help or his army's support. But not both.

Since Krishna had seen Arjuna first, he was given the first choice. Arjuna chose Krishna in spite of Krishna telling him that he would not himself fight.

Duryodhana was very happy. Krishna's army would fight on his side. He was sure he would win the war.

Krishna did not fight in the war between the Pandavas and the Kauravas. He was Arjuna's charioteer.

When Arjuna saw the Kaurava army—his cousins, uncles, teachers and friends—standing ready for battle, he refused to fight. But Krishna told him it was his duty to fight. He should fight for what was right.

All doubts cleared, Arjuna picked up his bow and went into battle.

Can you spot Hanuman?

For nine days, neither side won. Many rules of war were broken during this war. Krishna urged Arjuna to use any means to kill Bhishma, his great-uncle. Arjuna stood behind Shikhandi, a woman, and shot Bhishma. Bhishma fell.

After the Kauravas killed his son, Abhimanyu, Arjuna vowed to kill Jayadratha before sunset. When it was almost sunset and Arjuna had not found Jayadratha, he asked for Krishna's help.

Krishna covered the earth with a heavy fog. Thinking the sun had set, Jayadratha came out of hiding. Arjuna immediately shot him dead.

The war went on for eighteen days. With Krishna's help, the Pandavas won the war. But there was death and sadness all around.

Krishna went to see Gandhari, the blind-folded mother of the Kauravas, to beg forgiveness. But Gandhari was very angry and cursed Krishna, 'Your entire family will destroy itself and you will be alone, as I am alone.'

Finally Yudhishthira was crowned king. Krishna returned to Dwaraka.

But Gandhari's terrible curse did come true. And not only did Krishna's entire family kill each other, even the beautiful city of Dwaraka was submerged in the sea.

Krishna's work on earth was now over. He went into the forest and sat still under a banyan tree. A hunter thought Krishna's heel was the ear of a deer. He shot at it and thus Krishna met his end.

Ch1 143193 H